Happy: The Troll by The Yellow Door

Book 1

Imagined by Isabella and Tatyana Cruz

Written by Jackie Cruz

Illustrations by Mike Motz

Dedicated to Mom (Grandma), and our family and friends
(who are like family), for always being there for us.

To Ms. Ann, my favorite elementary school teacher,
for taking me to my first bookstore.

To the teachers and school staff that have been
and are a part of my girls' lives – thank you for all you do.

———————————◦⟨⟩◦———————————

One day while Isabella, Tatyana, and their mom were walking through their New York City neighborhood, the family came across a yellow door by the side of some stairs. At five years old, the girls, like all kids that age, had (and still have) an active imagination.

"Using your imagination, can you tell me a story about that door?" their mother asked. The girls nodded excitedly. Their mom leaned in to listen and the story began.

As two sisters took their afternoon walk in New York City, they were surprised to find a mysterious yellow door right there in their own neighborhood. As they walked closer, they thought they heard sobbing.

"Hello?" said Tatyana.

"Is there anyone in there?" asked Isabella.

"Just me," came a small voice from the other side of the door.

The girls were scared but curious, so they asked, "Are you okay? It sounds like you are crying."

The voice responded quietly, "I'm okay, but I'm cold. It rained last night, and my clothes got wet."

Not even giving it a second thought, Isabella took off her scarf and said, "I have a warm scarf for you. Do you want it?"

"Oh, yes," came the voice. "But the door is locked, and I am not allowed to go outside because the light bothers my eyes and is bad for me."

"If the door is locked, how do you get home?" asked Isabella.

"I live in a cave behind the door with my friends and family, but it is a secret and I will get in trouble if someone finds out that I am talking to you," came the response.

"How is it possible that there is a cave and you live in it?" asked Isabella.

"I am a troll," came the response, "and trolls, fairies, elves, gargoyles, and all kinds of creatures have been living in these caves for centuries."

The girls were even more curious, but they knew that even if the door were open, they should never go into a dark, unknown place.

Tatyana thought they should leave, but before she could say anything, Isabella said, "Well, I have this scarf for you and since the door is closed, I will go ahead and put it through the slots in the door."

As Isabella put the scarf through, they noticed that it was also being pulled from the inside. Once the scarf was completely through, they heard laughter.

"Thank you so much for this beautiful scarf! It will definitely keep me warm, and I love it!" said the voice joyfully.

"You're welcome," said Isabella, pleased with herself for being able to help.

The girls and the troll had many questions about each other and spent some time talking. The troll told them how he and the other creatures came from a place called "Tersah." Only Tersians knew of their existence and it was rare for them to speak with humans. The girls were fascinated, but it was getting late and Tatyana thought that they should be leaving.

Before they left, they asked the troll for its name.

"I don't have a human name; I have a troll name, and it may be hard for you to pronounce," said the Troll, adding, "All Trolls are also given nicknames after an area or where they usually can be found – Tersians call me 'the troll by the yellow door.'"

The girls thought about that, and Isabella said, "Is it okay if we call you 'Happy: The Troll by the Yellow Door'? Because before you were sad, and now you sound happy."

"I like that," Happy responded and excitedly proclaimed, "I am Happy: the troll by the yellow door."

Tatyana, Isabella, and Happy then said their goodbyes and promised to talk to each other again.

The girls kept their promise and would stop and talk to Happy whenever they could.

Weeks later, the girls were out around dusk and were walking a short distance from the yellow door when they thought they heard laughter. Happy had told them that when the sun went down, and as long as no one was around, the trolls came out to play.

The girls did not see any trolls, but they could imagine them running through the overgrown area, swinging from the grates that were there and playing hide and seek in some of the passages in-between the various buildings.

Tatyana said, "Listen! That must be the trolls playing."

"Shhh," said Isabella "We are not supposed to know about the trolls; it's a secret."

So as not to give away the secret, the girls slowly kept walking. "I wish we could see them," said Isabella. "In my mind and based on what Happy told us, I can just picture what he looks like; I would love to be able to see or meet him in person even for a few minutes."

"That would take us being out late at night since Happy can't be out during the day, and we are still too young for that," said Tatyana.

Just then the girls thought they saw some of the bushes by them moving, but because they did not want to get Happy in trouble they whispered, "Happy, if you can hear us, we hope you have a great time playing. We think of you every time we walk this way and will stop by the door to talk to you soon."

There was an extra little rustle in the nearest bush, and the girls knew that Happy had heard them. They smiled at each and continued walking.

Time went by and the girls always said, "Hi, Happy," or "Have a great day, Happy" when they walked past the yellow door. If no one was around, they would stop and talk to him, but it was mostly quick so as not to get Happy in trouble or the trolls discovered.

One Saturday while walking by the door, the girls heard Happy say, "I've been waiting for you. I have a surprise for you. You can now see what I look like. Just go up the stairs and follow the yellow ball."

Confused, the girls asked what Happy was talking about.

Happy repeated his request that they find the yellow ball and by the sound of his voice, they could tell he was excited about something.

The girls shouted their agreement and eagerly ran up the stairs. They weren't exactly sure what form the "yellow ball" would take, so they kept their eyes peeled for anything that might be it.

Suddenly, about halfway up, Isabella noticed a Pac-Man painted on the side of the stairs.

"Could this be it?" Isabella asked Tatyana.

"I don't know," said Tatyana, "but it looks like the Pac-Man is leading us to this yard behind this fence and under these buildings."

"What could this mean?" said Isabella, still confused.

The girls started looking through the fence, trying to figure out what they were supposed to find.

Just then the sun shifted, and they noticed that all the way at the back left-hand side of the yard, carved into one of the massive stone stilts that were holding up the building, was what looked like a statue.

The statue looked to be about medium height, not too big and not too small. It had a long nose, big cheeks, and appeared to be smiling. His arms hung down beside him with his feet together as if proudly standing at attention.

"What is that?" asked Tatyana to no one in particular.

"Is that what we are supposed to find?" said Isabella aloud.

"Yes, that is it," said Happy from somewhere nearby. "A few weeks ago I was playing outside with my friends and I heard you wondering what I looked like, so I carved a statue so that you could see me."

The girls wanted to say so much, but all that came out of their mouths was, "Wow, that's amazing."

They could not believe that Happy had taken the time to carve a statue for them.

"Tersians are master craftspeople," Happy said proudly. "For example, we are excellent cooks, builders, and, believe it or not, gargoyles are great at watching children. Just look up when you are walking and you will see gargoyle statues looking down at everyone, watching."

The girls had many questions for Happy, and they spent some time just talking and learning more about their new friend. They also taught Happy about humans. (Even though he was hundreds of years old, there were some things he had questions about.)

Happy let them know that when they were older and could come out at night they could play together; but for now, even though they could not actually see him, they had the statue to show them exactly what he looked like.

"My Godmother is calling me," said Happy sometime later.

"Is she a fairy?" asked Isabella.

Letting out a loud laugh Happy said, "That's a long story. I will tell you about her another time."

The girls also laughed, and in that moment, they were all happy.

That night the girls learned two things: You never know where you are going to make a new friend, **and** (even more incredible) is that trolls, fairies, gargoyles, elves – all fairytale creatures really exist.

The End

Preview of Book 2:

It had been a year since the girls had met Happy and they spent as much time with him as possible. They still had not been able to meet him face to face, but they had the statue, and that was enough for now.

One day Tatyana and Isabella were in a car heading towards downtown Manhattan when they looked up and noticed gargoyles carved into the side of a building. They thought about what Happy had told them and waved up at the statues.

At that moment, they thought they noticed one of the statues move. Surprised Isabella asked, "Did you see that?"

"Uh-huh," responded Tatyana, looking up with her eyes as wide as can be. They immediately had a sense that something was wrong. Later that night they would find out that they were right.

A Note from Mommy

There is a whole world of wonder waiting for you!
Don't be afraid to dream and to use your imagination,
and especially do not be surprised if one day you find
your "Happy" friend too.

Keeping it Real

The world of Happy the Troll is based on the imaginative stories that Isabella and Tatyana created while enjoying the very real places in our own neighborhood. Each scene in this book is based on real locations, which we've recreated in the various illustrations. We hope you enjoy sharing our day with us and the fun stories that we've created for you along the way. Over the next few pages, we've shared a few snapshots of the places that inspired us!

Photo by: Pattie McNab

Meet the Authors

Isabella and Tatyana are 6-year-old twins:

Tatyana Cruz is an inquisitive child whose favorite words are who, what, where, when, and why. She loves adventure, and when outside, can be found climbing anything she can, running, and playing.

Isabella Cruz is a creative child who is energetic and focused. She loves to take her time and observe before she explores and asks questions, which makes her our perfect storyteller.

Jackie Cruz is the proud mom of these young ladies. When not working in Human Resources, she loves to be adventurous and creative. She sees different aspects of herself in her girls and has no doubt that they are her greatest loves and Masterpieces.

Lightning Source UK Ltd.
Milton Keynes UK
UKHW050634300420
362540UK00005B/13